Samuel French Acting Edition

The Ballad of King Windowglass

by Jack Kurtz

SAMUELFRENCH.COM   SAMUELFRENCH.CO.UK

For Production Enquiries

United States and Canada
Info@SamuelFrench.com
1-866-598-8449

United Kingdom and Europe
Plays@SamuelFrench.co.uk
020-7255-4302

Each title is subject to availability from Samuel French, depending upon country of performance. Please be aware that *THE BALLAD OF KING WINDOWGLASS* may not be licensed by Samuel French in your territory. Professional and amateur producers should contact the nearest Samuel French office or licensing partner to verify availability.

Please refer to page 33 for further copyright information.

Dedicated to David
Who did a great job with the King.

CHARACTERS

The Quartette
Two Peasants
King Wenceslas
Scruffy
The Poor Man
Sir Ewing the Inept
Sister Antagonistica
Burgher Morgan of Avarice on the Rhine
The Bureaucrat

BALLAD OF KING WINDOWGLASS

(Open bare stage or chancel, except that Upstage Left is a single leafless tree with sign crudely drawn in crayon reading "Forust." QUARTETTE enters. They are dressed in traditional Dickensian fashion. They take their place somewhere where they can see the action and be seen by the audience but are not in the action, e.g. on floor level or behind a choir rail. Very cheerfully with somewhat phony "carol singing" style, they do first verse of "Good King Wenceslas.")

QUARTETTE.
Good King Wenceslas looked out,
On the feast of Stephen,
When the snow lay round about,
Deep and crisp and even.
Brightly shone the moon that night,
Though the frost was cruel,
When a poor man came in sight,
Gath'ring winter fuel.

(Stage LIGHTS come up blue. SOUNDS of blizzard. Two "PEASANTS" struggle on stage, fighting the wind, stop Stage Left.)

PEASANT ONE. *(Peering off Right, then pointing and shouting above the wind.)* Ho! Look yon. Someone cometh.
PEASANT TWO. Ho, whither?
ONE. Yon.
TWO. Yon? I seeth naught yon.

ONE. Just a little over from yon toward thither.

TWO. Oh. Yea, verily. I see him now. Thither.

ONE. Closer to yon.

TWO. Thither.

ONE. He's moved. He was yon when I first mentioned it.

TWO. No matter.

ONE. Who, ho?

TWO. I knoweth not. The knave is too far thither.

ONE. Yon.

TWO. Forget it.

ONE. Ho. He draws nigh. Methinks I recognize yon pilgrim.

TWO. Ho, who?

ONE. Methinks it is the king.

TWO. Good King Wendleglance, uh, Wearyloose, uh, Weasleschlause.

ONE. Wenceslas.

TWO. Whatever.

ONE. Prithee, why would the King be abroad on such a night as this?

TWO. Aye. Though "Brightly shines the moon this night," still "the snow lies round about, Deep and crisp and even."

ONE. "And the frost is cru-el."

TWO. Cruel.

ONE. Whatever.

TWO. Indeed, what twisted web of circumstance might bring the king forth on such a night?

ONE. What crisis to the land, what threat or hope for the body politic, might bring the king forth on such a night?

TWO. What casting of the runes of fickle fate wouldst propel his high-born epidermis into this cru-el blizzard?

BOTH. What, ho? (*Pause.*) Oh-ho.

(KING WENCESLAS enters jogging, in jogging suit and crown. Runs in place Stage Center holding one end of tape measure while SCRUFFY, winding up tape, catches up with him.)

ONE. I thought he was looking a little pudgy at his last press conference.

WENCESLAS. How much further, page, 'ere I reach my goal?

SCRUFFY. Yet some four hundred roods, my Lord.

WENCESLAS. *(Panting.)* If King Thermoguard can do it, I can do it. Measure on, page.

SCRUFFY. *(Handing WENCESLAS one end of the tape.)* Yes, my Lord. *(SCRUFFY goes offstage with tape to measure King's run.)*

PEASANTS. *(Bowing, speaking together.)* Hail Good King . . .

Peasant Two. *(Simultaneously.)* . . .Wenceslas.

Peasant One. *(Simultaneously.)* . . .Whatever.

WENCESLAS. *(Panting.)* Good even', loyal subjects. *(Glancing off Right.)* What Ho? E'en on this cru-el night, there wanders abroad another of my faithful subjects. See, he comes yon.

TWO. Thither.

WENCESLAS. *(Somewhat threateningly.)* Yon.

BOTH. Yon.

ONE. Methinks he is a poor man who comes in sight. *(POOR MAN enters, begins to collect sticks and put them into a burlap bag.)*

TWO. Gathering winter fu-u-el.

WENCESLAS. Fuel.

TWO. *(Shrugging.)* It's your kingdom. *(POOR MAN proceeds to gather fuel, including a can of propane gas and a sack of charcoal briquets.)*

WENCESLAS. (*Calling off Left.*) Oh Scruffy!
SCRUFFY. (*Entering, panting.*) Yes, my Lord?
WENCESLAS. I have a question for you. (*Shouting.*)
FREEZE! (*All ACTORS freeze in place during song.*)
QUARTETTE.
"Hither, page and stand by me,
If thou knows't it telling,
Yonder peasant, who is he?
Where and what his dwelling?'
"Sir, he lives a good league hence,
Underneath the mountain,
Right against the forest fence,
By Saint Agnes' fountain."

(*During this time POOR MAN exits.*)

WENCESLAS. (*All break poses.*) Where did he go?
SCRUFFY. I think he left during the second verse.
WENCESLAS. My heart is moved by his sad plight. There,
but for accident of fate and birth go I. Can I not but see on this
Holy night that our positions are so chosen by the hand of God
that I might show munificence? FREEZE! (*All ACTORS
freeze in place during song.*)
QUARTETTE.
"Bring me flesh, and bring me wine,
Bring me pine logs hither;
Thou and I shall see him dine,
When we bear them thither."
WENCESLAS. Home to the pantry. (*They go off.*)
ONE. Let us, too, go thither.
TWO. Yes, thither. (*THEY exit in opposite directions.
Dialogue from Offstage Left.*)

WENCESLAS. This cold night that poor man shall dine in splendor as a king. That sack, Scruffy. Fill it. The wild boar.

SCRUFFY. Yes, my Lord.

WENCESLAS. Truffles, pheasant, plum pudding. Some of that. Seven of those. No, you idiot, the plum pudding goes on top. Ugh.

SCRUFFY. Sorry, my Lord.

WENCESLAS. Some of that. No, more. A great deal of that.

SCRUFFY. My Lord.

WENCESLAS. A dozen of those. Six cans of that. Uh, throw in that little whatchamajigee that you turn upside down and then it snoweth.

SCRUFFY. My Lord.

WENCESLAS. No. Leave out the whatchamajigee. I've hardly had a chance to play with it myself.

SCRUFFY. My Lord.

WENCESLAS. Now then, we'll need a great deal of that. Some of those. Four or five of those. A lot of that.

SCRUFFY. My Lord.

WENCESLAS. Now then. I shalt lead the way, and you carry the sack.

SCRUFFY. MY LORD! (*THEY enter with SCRUFFY carrying an enormous sack. They proceed to Stage Center.*)

WENCESLAS. FREEZE! (*ALL freeze in place during song.*)

QUARTETTE.

Page and monarch, forth they went,

Forth they went together;

Through the rude wind's wild lament

And the bitter weather.

(*As they sing, SCRUFFY, grimacing, slowly collapses under the weight of the sack.*)

WENCESLAS. How much further, Scruffy? (*No answer.*)
Scruffy? (*Turns.*) Scruffy? (*Hand comes out from under sack,
waves weakly.*) Look, boy, when I say freeze, I mean freeze.
(*Pulling him from under sack.*) (*Looking off Left.*) What ho?
A rider coming hither . . . from thither.

SCRUFFY. (*Peering.*) Out of the night . . . a knight.
(*WENCESLAS gives him a dirty look. He shrugs. KNIGHT
enters, riding stick horse.*) Methinks it is your faithful servant,
Baron of all the fiefdom of Middle Management, the bold and
fearless Sir Ewing the Inept.

WENCESLAS. Ho, Sir Ewing.

EWING.   (*He dismounts, kneels, kisses WENCESLAS'
hand.*) Your humble servant, oh Good King Wienerslop.

WENCESLAS. Wenceslas.

EWING. Whatever.

WENCESLAS.   Rise and tell us of your quests and
pilgrimages. It has been fair many a night since your golden
countenance has graced the gay roistering of our firelit halls.
Whither beenest thou?

EWING.   Oh, Good, my Lord, I have been abroad
throughout the kingdom, slaying fair maidens and rescuing
dragons.

SCRUFFY.   That's slaying dragons and rescuing fair
maidens.

EWING. (*Turns to audience with puzzled look on his face
which changes to gradual comprehension and finally a grimace
of frustration. HE snaps fingers.*) Darn.

WENCESLAS. Well, maybe next time.

EWING. (*During the speech that follows, EWING draws his
sword, and delivers the speech with much posturing and waving
of the sword, putting the KING and SCRUFFY in frequent*

danger from his random swings.) I have also been fighting injustice, championing the poor and the powerless. I have placed life itself at risk in the cause of the overthrow of the tyrannous establishment . . . How was your day? (*SCRUFFY is slowing sinking into the ground under the bag.*)

WENCESLAS. My heart has been sore moved to pity by the sight of a poor man gathering winter fu-u-el, and I have betaken myself to make generous offer of provender of flesh, wine, and pine logs, wherewith e'en now I bring them to his humble cottage in yon sack carried by yon page. (*He turns.*) Scruffy? (*SCRUFFY waves hand from under sack. WENCESLAS pulls him up.*)

EWING. Oh, Good My Lord, may your humble vassal be so bold as to speak words of chastisement to my liege?

WENCESLAS. What ho?

EWING. (*More posturing and sword swinging.*) Although I know your heart is pure and stirred with pity, you do in fact do injustice to this poor man. Your gift is paternalistic. This poor man is not so much wanting in material things, but is a victim of the system.

WENCESLAS. What ho?

EWING. (*More posturing and sword swinging.*) It is not gifts that he needs, but justice. Not some temporary respite from his cruel lot, but a new political and economic system. (*After a particularly close miss, WENCELSLAS grabs EWING'S sword arm and firmly takes sword from him.*) Throw down thy patronizing sack, and join me in the battle against injustice. Throw thy heart and body into the battle to overthrow the tyrannous establishment.

WENCESLAS. Say what?

EWING. The tyrannous establishment. All who crush the poor with bitter burdens. All who pitilessly prey upon the peasants in their penurious poverty.

SCRUFFY. Not bad. (*Or, if he doesn't manage it, "Better luck next time.*")

WENCESLAS. Ewing, boy.

EWING. Yes, my Lord?

WENCESLAS. Are you not Lord of all of the Barony of Middle Management?

EWING. Oh yes, my Lord, by your munificent grace.

WENCESLAS. And as Baron, do you not reap the harvest of a hundred fields tended by a thousand peasants? Do you not command the allegiance of a thousand yeoman soldiers? Do you not collect the taxes of the craftsmen of a dozen towns?

EWING. Yes, my Lord. That's pretty much what the Baron business is all about. Oh good my Lord, join me in the overthrow of the tyrannous establishment.

WENCESLAS. Is not your castle maintained by a good gross of maids, footmen, stable boys, gardeners, and serving wenches?

EWING. Why yes, good my Lord. Oh, I would that you might see my vision and join me in the fight against the tyrannous establishment.

WENCESLAS. Ewing . . .

EWING. Yes, my Lord.

WENCESLAS. You are the tyrannous establishment.

EWING. (*Face to audience, same progression from surprise through puzzlement to chagrin. Snaps fingers.*) Darn!

WENCESLAS. And one more thing. Am I not King over a hundred barons and do not I, from you, expect loyalty, fealty, and 32% of the gross?

EWING. Yes, my Lord.

WENCESLAS. (*Grabbing him by the collar and lifting him until he stands on tiptoe.*) THEN I MUST BE THE

TYRANNOUS ESTABLISHMENT!!!!

EWING. (*Looking out at audience.*) No one ever explained it to me quite that way.

WENCESLAS. Then I think you'd best get back to your fair maidens and your dragons.

EWING. Your word is my command. (*He mounts his "horse" and rides off. As he goes, in the manner of one trying to get it fixed in his memory.*) Slay dragons, rescue maidens. Slay dragons, rescue maidens. Slay dragons, rescue maidens. (*He is off.*)

WENCESLAS. And yet, methinks, there is some truth in what he says. Somehow it dampens the joy I felt but moments ago. Still, for now, good page, we will proceed. (*They begin walking in place again.*)

SCRUFFY. (*Pointing.*) Yon.

WENCESLAS. Another of my subjects on this cru-el night.

SCRUFFY. More or less. It is methinks, Sister Antagonistica, Prioress of the Sweet Little Sisters of Sentimental Slop.

SISTER. (*Entering.*) Ho, Good King Whiffleschnapps.

WENCESLAS. Wenceslas.

SISTER. Whatever. What kingly errand brings thee forth on such a night?

WENCESLAS. My heart has been sore moved to pity by the sight of a poor man gathering winter fu-el, and I have betaken myself to make generous offer of provender of flesh, wine, and pine logs, wherewith e'en now I bring them to his humble cottage. Sister, wilt thou bless me in this undertaking of simple charity? (*He kneels.*)

SISTER. Simple? (*Patting him on the head.*) Little is as simple as we might sometimes want it to be. Have you, mayhap, examined your motivation?

WENCESLAS. Huh?

SISTER. Do you really wish to give provender to this poor man from simple charity, or is it only a response to your hidden guilt feelings?

WENCESLAS. Huh?

SISTER. Are you moved by altruism, by real concern for this poor man, or do you seek thanks, his groveling appreciation, does the act proceed from a desire for your own feelings of personal satisfaction?

WENCESLAS. (*He stands.*) Well, I hadn't . . .

SISTER. Do you seek the benefit of another, or do you seek only the approval and admiration of your peers, fame, reputation, perhaps a carol written about your good deed?

WENCESLAS. Well . . .

SISTER. Examine not the act, Good King, but the motivation behind the act. Then, and only then, will I grant you blessing.

WENCESLAS. Well, I'll think about it and check with you next Sunday.

SISTER. Good. (*Pulls out tambourine.*) Little something for the church? (*WENCESLAS drops bag of coins into tambourine, and SISTER exits jiggling tambourine and crying "Alms. Alms for the Poor."*)

WENCESLAS. Could it be that I know not my own mind? What say you, Scruffy? (*Turning, SCRUFFY is under the bag.*) Scruffy? (*Pulls him up.*) Should we, mayhap, return to the palace (*SCRUFFY shakes head vigorously "yes."*) where I might have opportunity to consider at leisure the workings of my heart, to meditate upon the deepest recesses of my soul? But no, that would only cause one poor man to spend more nights in cold and hunger. We shall press on, although my heart is sorely troubled now. Pray that we meet no more gentle folk who might question our once clear path.

SCRUFFY. Too late.

WENCESLAS. Yon?

SCRUFFY. Thither.

WENCESLAS. Ho.

SCRUFFY. Good Burger Morgan of Avarice on the Rhine.

WENCESLAS. Do you think he hath seen us?

SCRUFFY. 'Fraid so.

MORGAN. What ho, Good King Mooseburger.

WENCESLAS. Mooseburger?

SCRUFFY. Wenceslas.

MORGAN. Whatever.

WENCESLAS. How do you get Mooseburger out of Wenceslas?

MORGAN. Hail to the King, maintainer of order and patron of economic growth.

WENCESLAS. Hail, Morgan. What brings you forth on such a night?

MORGAN. Pursuit of justice.

WENCESLAS. We've had that one.

MORGAN. Foreclosing a mortgage on Widow Schnivel.

WENCESLAS. Oh.

MORGAN. And you, Good King?

WENCESLAS. Oh, uh, just out for a stroll.

MORGAN. On such a night? Cru-el wind and all that?

WENCESLAS. Improveth the circulation.

MORGAN. And what carrieth yon page in yon great sack?

WENCESLAS. Oh, uh, just a little something for a late snack. Little hot chocolate, donut or two . . .

SCRUFFY. (*Collapsing under sack.*) Give it up! Tell him! Tell him!

WENCESLAS. Well, actually (*Rapidly and without inflection since he just wants to get it over with.*) my heart has been sore moved to pity by the sight of a poor man gathering winter fu-el, and I have betaken myself to make generous offer of flesh, wine, and pine logs, wherewith e'en now I bring them to his humble cottage.

MORGAN. Shame!

WENCESLAS. Here goeth we again.

MORGAN. Knowest not that to giveth to the poor only maketh them more dependent and slothful? Knowest not that they have no appreciation for the finer things in life? Give them decent homes and they will neglect them unto rack and ruin. Shouldst thou provide stereos, they will only play the Beach Boys (or pick your own rock group.) Shouldst thou bring them bathtubs, they will use them only to ferment mead for drunken debauches.

WENCESLAS. We aren't bringing a bathtub.

SCRUFFY. (*Crawling up over the sack.*) Yes, we are. It's about half way down in the sack. You had me put it in right after the second plum pudding. (*Realization, hits head.*) Uh-oh.

WENCESLAS. (*Looking in sack.*) Yuck.

MORGAN. The poor are poor because they waste their money. Every one of them haveth Cadillac carts. Look down in yon valley at the homes of the peasants. On every hovel roof standeth a television antenna. What a waste.

SCRUFFY. (*Shouldering sack.*) Especially since it's going to be about a thousand years before they can buy television sets.

MORGAN. All peasants are inherently stupid and lazy. (*To SCRUFFY.*) You, churl, droppeth that sack.

SCRUFFY. Right. (*He drops it on MORGAN'S foot.*)

MORGAN. AHHHHHHHHHHHHHHH! My foot, my foot, take it off!

SCRUFFY. Right. (*Pulls knife.*) Above or below the knee?

MORGAN. The sack, the sack. Take the sack off, you idiot. (*SCRUFFY hoists sack.*)

SCRUFFY. Sorry. It's my inherent peasant stupidity.

MORGAN. Surely, Sire, you do not intend to go on with this folly of yours?

WENCESLAS. Right now, Good Burger, my intent is to deliver this sack against even the most heinous odds. If we must travel seven seasons, we shall deliver it. If we must cross great mountain ranges, we will deliver it. If we must ford rivers clogged with ice floes, we will deliver it. (*SCRUFFY is sinking under sack again with pitiful look on face.*)

MORGAN. But thou knowest not how thy gift will be usedeth.

WENCESLAS. I figure he'll eat it. Except the logs and the bathtub.

MORGAN. But once eaten, thy gift will be transformed into energy, and, with additional energy, who knows what vile things a peasant might do? Thou hast no control over thy gift.

WENCESLAS. We will press on.

MORGAN. Then may the unrealistically raised expectations of the poor be on thy head. (*He huffs off.*)

WENCESLAS. Quickly, Scruffy. (*They trudge.*) My heart is sore downcast. Knowest thou some way to cheer it? (*SCRUFFY reaches in the bag, hands him small snow dome. He plays with it awhile. Begins to chuckle.*) Fascinating. I wonder what marvelous sorcery makes it work?

SCRUFFY. Gravity.

WENCESLAS. Have they invented that?

SCRUFFY. Not yet.

WENCESLAS. Oh.

BUREAUCRAT. Oh, yoo hoo, King!

WENCESLAS. Oh, no. Hurry, Scruffy. (*They run in place.*)

BUREAUCRAT. (*Approaching them.*) Oh, Sire, my heart doth rejoice that I have overtaken thee.

WENCESLAS. (*They're still running in place.*) Do you suppose we're doing this wrong?

BUREAUCRAT. I cometh from the Royal Bureau of Economic Stimulation and Peasant Relief. Word didst reach us that thou sought to give a boon to the poor, and it was our fear that thou mightest not know of the matching funds plan.

WENCESLAS. (*Both stop running.*) Matching funds?

BUREAUCRAT. Yea, verily. If thou givest a private gift to the poor, our bureau will provide in kind.

WENCESLAS. Finally, someone who understandeth.

BUREAUCRAT. Provided the gift meeteth certain criteria. Is that the gift in yon sack?

WENCESLAS. (*Wary.*) Uh, yes.

BUREAUCRAT. (*Peering into sack.*) Now then, what are you charging for all of this?

WENCESLAS. Charging?

BUREAUCRAT. Yes. We need to know if the cost includes a fair percentage of the overhead for the rest of the castle. (*She looks in the sack and begins to rummage round in it.*)

WENCESLAS. Well, I'd really planned to . . .

BUREAUCRAT. Oh, my goodness. (*Looking up from the sack.*) Now really, Good King Whittleplace . . .

WENCESLAS. Wenceslas.

BUREAUCRAT. Whatever. You have a wild boar in here.

WENCESLAS. So?

BUREAUCRAT. Are you aware that scientific studies have shown that wild boar has almost no nutritional value?

SCRUFFY. Neither does a bathtub.

BUREAUCRAT. I'm afraid there's one other thing. This peasant, he is a male Czechoslovakian?

SCRUFFY. Yeah.

BUREAUCRAT. Have you within the past thirty days provided, or do you intend to within the next thirty days, provide an equivalent gift for a female Lithuanian?

WENCESLAS. No, but I beginneth to get certain thoughts as to what I will do in the next thirty seconds.

BUREAUCRAT. Now then, we haveth a few forms to filleth out for the family survey. (*She brings out enormous batch of forms.*) We needeth these in triplicate.

WENCESLAS. HOLDETH IT!

BUREAUCRAT. Sire, there are certain rules.

WENCESLAS. I changeth them.

BUREAUCRAT. Thou canst not . . . I guess thou canst. Now the forms . . .

WENCESLAS. I AM THE KING!

BUREAUCRAT. Now that I thinketh on it, maybe one of our typists could . . .

WENCESLAS. Thou hast thirty seconds to exist somewhere else. (*She scurries off.*) ONWARD! (*They trudge.*) FREEZE! (*They do.*)

QUARTETTE. (*They are starting to get a little discouraged by what they have seen and they are singing a little more slowly and with less enthusiasm. At the appropriate line, WENCESLAS and SCRUFFY being to trudge again, SCRUFFY trying to walk in the King's footsteps as stated in the song.*)
"Sire, the night is darker now,
And the wind grows stronger;
Fails my heart, I know not how;
I can go no longer."

"Mark my footsteps, my good page,
Tread thou in them boldly;
Thou shalt find the winter's rage
Freeze thy blood less coldly,"
    SCRUFFY. (*After a few more seconds of walking in the King's footprints.*) It doesn't help a great deal, you know.
    WENCESLAS. Darkness is upon my soul.
    SCRUFFY. Frozenness is upon my body. (*They struggle offstage, right back on. SCRUFFY, totally exhausted, crawling on his stomach dragging the sack.*)
    SCRUFFY. Sire, ahead. Look.
    WENCESLAS. Thither?
    SCRUFFY. There! Is that where he lives? There. Right against the forest fence, underneath the mountain.
    WENCESLAS. I think that's the entrance to the new channel tunnel.
    SCRUFFY. No, a little more toward yon.
    WENCESLAS. Yes. I see it. I see it. PEASANT! PEASANT! (*Both begin to shout.*)
    PEASANT. (*Enters, takes sack.*) What kept you? (*Exits. SCRUFFY just lies there while WENCESLAS stares after the PEASANT, dumbfounded.*)
    QUARTETTE. (*Totally disgusted, they are singing slowly without enthusiasm and with more than few sour notes.*)
In his master's steps he trod,
Where the snow lay dinted;
Heat was in the very sod
Which the saint had printed.
Therefore, Christian men, be sure,
Wealth or rank possessing,
Ye who now will bless the poor,
Shall yourselves find blessing.

(During last two lines, WENCESLAS and SCRUFFY trudge off, discouraged. At end of verse, QUARTETTE follows them. LIGHTS fade out. They come back up, white.   SCRUFFY enters, carrying a throne, WENCESLAS follows and sits in it. SCRUFFY exits. He returns carrying scroll.)

SCRUFFY. Uh, canst thou bring to mind last St. Stephen's feast and a poor man whom thou feedest?

WENCESLAS. Forsooth, at least a thank you note.

SCRUFFY. Not exactly. *(Looking at scroll.)* It seems the roast boar may have been a little ill-preserved. He got food poisoning. He's suing you.

WENCESLAS. *(Out of throne in a towering rage.)* I AM THE KING! I AM GOOD KING WINDOWGLASS!

SCRUFFY. Wenceslas.

WENCESLAS. WHATEVER! *(He collapses in chair. A puzzled and slightly demented look comes on his face, and he begins to mumble.)* Windowglass? No. Whittleshift? No. *(SCRUFFY shrugs and exits.)* Wilburslough? No. I know it as well as I know my own name. Wanklebrat? Fred? Harry? Glen? Rocky? Ewell? . . . *(As LIGHTS fade out.)*

THE END

(OR . . .)

EITHER OF THE TWO OPTIONAL EPILOGUES WHICH FOLLOW MAY BE USED WITH THE PLAY UNDER DIFFERENT CIRCUMSTANCES OF PRODUCTION.

If the play is done in a church or by a religious group, the author recommends the first optional epilogue. The second optional epilogue is recommended for a secular setting, only if you simply must have a more positive ending.

* * * * * * * * * *

FIRST OPTIONAL EPILOGUE

(The parts in the epilogue below may be played by the same actors and actresses who appeared in the play proper. They should quickly remove their partial costumes and do it in ordinary clothing. "The King of Heaven and Earth" should be played by the same actor who did Wenceslas. Or, if you have lots of other people who want parts, you can work with an entire second cast.

LIGHTS come up on bare stage with "The King of Heaven and Earth" seated on the throne from the previous scene with the "heavenly host" arranged randomly around him. The NARRATOR stands Downstage to the extreme Left.)

NARRATOR. Better, perhaps, not to even try, not to even give gifts. Wenceslas probably didn't really have that much trouble, and normally we don't either. But sometimes . . . Gifts can be misunderstood, misused, and -- worst of all? -- unappreciated. We have an epilogue to the play. Or, more properly, a prologue which comes at the end. There was once a King of Heaven and Earth. Some two thousand years ago, as we measure time, he called an audience for the members of his court.

KING. I have looked at my Kingdom below. So many hate and hurt, so many are in need while others find no happiness in riches. I have determined that it is the right time. I am going to give the gift.

FIRST SPEAKER. (*After hesitation.*) My Lord, I know you do it out of love, but I would ask you to consider the consequences. I warn you that if you give the gift, many will not see it as an act of love, but as a threat to their freedom.

KING. I know.

SECOND SPEAKER. I see, as well, that some will refuse the gift, will laugh at it and at those who do accept it.

KING. I know.

THIRD SPEAKER. But, My Lord, even some who do accept the gift will pervert it. A few will even torture and kill in the name of the gift.

KING. I know. It is the way they are.

FOURTH SPEAKER. Some will use the gift to claim superiority over others. Some will use the gift only to gain power and wealth.

FIFTH SPEAKER. And many, Lord, many will claim acceptance of the gift, but treat it cheaply, showing no real gratitude or response.

KING. I know these things. I have considered them. They are a part of my pain. Still, this year, in Bethlehem, I will give the gift. And not all of what follows will be what I want. It is the risk one takes in giving a gift. But if I chose not to do it, they would be alone.

NARRATOR. And so The King of Heaven and Earth gave the gift. And each did with it what was pleasing in his own sight. And we still do. Amen.

THE END

(OR)

* * * * *

SECOND OPTIONAL EPILOGUE

(Open on original setting with the tree and the sign, "Forust." The NARRATOR, who may be one of the cast members from the main play who has removed his or her partial costume, stands Downstage on the extreme Left.)

NARRATOR. Better, perhaps, not to even try, not to even give gifts. Wenceslas probably didn't really have that much trouble, and normally we don't either. But sometimes . . . Gifts can be misunderstood, misused, and -- worst of all? -- unappreciated. But if we stopped giving gifts, what would be lost to the world? Sometimes we never really know.

(The POOR MAN slouches onstage, dragging the sack, chuckling with an evil grin of satisfaction on his face. A "WOODLAND CREATURE," another actor or actress, partially costumed as a rabbit or squirrel or whatever you can easily come up with, comes limping Onstage from the other side and collapses in an exhausted and starving heap, panting and whimpering. The PEASANT looks at the animal with only vague interest. Then he begins to look back and forth from the animal to his sack with increasing concern. Finally, somewhat reluctantly, he reaches into the sack and pulls out a head of lettuce (or whatever). Gives it to the animal. The ANIMAL chews on it, a smile of bliss

comes across its face and it hugs The POOR MAN. The ANIMAL exits. Gradually a smile of real satisfaction and joy appears on the face of the PEASANT who winds up facing directly out at the audience.)

NARRATOR. When we give a gift, sometimes we never really know . . . (*LIGHTS fade out.*)

THE END

PRODUCTION NOTES

THE CAST

The Ballad of King Windowglass was originally written to be performed by Junior High Youth. It has since been done by a number of different groups ranging from older elementary children to adults. The author was particularly surprised and pleased when he received a request for permission to perform the play from a drama group at a retirement community in Florida.

Some of the parts may be cast as either men or women (boys or girls). The part of Scruffy was written for a boy but has been portrayed by a girl. The bureaucrat has been both male and female. The two peasants at the beginning may obviously be of either gender. In a pinch, Sister Antagonistica of the Sweet Little Sisters of Sentimental Slop could become Brother Antagonistica of, say, The Benevolent Brothers of Pompous Piety.

In general, Scruffy should be younger (or at least smaller) than the other cast members.

THE QUARTETTE

In the original production, although the cast was junior high youth, the quartette were adults, a mixed quartette of trained singers who did a very professional job singing the carol in harmony, at least at the first. Of course if you don't have trained singers available and/or you have a lot of people who tried out for whom you don't have parts, The Quartette can become The Carolers, and can sing in unison if necessary. The show is, however, enhanced, if the singing is really good at the beginning in order to contrast with the ending.

The Quartette, or group of carolers, stands to the side where they can be seen by the audience but not interfere with the action of the play. They watch what is happening and during the course of the King's travails, they become increasingly disillusioned, perhaps whispering silently to each other occasionally. (Be careful that they don't become overly enthusiastic about this and distract from the play.) By the end the quality of the singing has degenerated considerably as the singers "just want to finish this and get out of here."

THE SET

The author is told that some groups have put together rather elaborate sets for the production. Personally, I prefer it simple- -bare stage, chancel, or just about any flat area that can be seen by the audience. The tree should be about six or seven feet tall, completely devoid of leaves, and set in a standard home-made Christmas tree stand of braced boards, probably leaning. The sign that hangs on the tree should be in crayon, misspelled with at least one letter reversed, reading "Forust," or possibly "Forest Primevul." The "throne" should be some kind of "boardroom" chair or possibly a pulpit chair.

COSTUMING

Some groups have done the show in full medieval costuming. The author prefers "partial" costuming, combining contemporary clothing with medieval accessories. The accessories may be very simple. There is no need for them to be particularly authentic. The original cast was costumed as follows.

PEASANTS - Levis and sweat shirts (possibly with "good

old boy" messages of some kind on them) and pointed peasant caps.

KING WENCESLAS - He wears a jogging suit and crown when he first appears. When he reappears to deliver the sack, he has added a long gold cape over the jogging suit.

SCRUFFY - Levis, tennis shoes, a simple jerkin, and a page's cap.

SIR EWING - Levis, plastic knight's helmet and breast plate, if available, and short cape.

SISTER ANTAGONISTICA - Simple dress, black wimple, possibly a black cape.

BURGHER MORGAN - Business suit with long, fake-fur trimmed black cape.

BUREAUCRAT - Simple dress or slack suit and one of those long pointed hats with the wispy streamers coming out of the top. (I don't know what they're called, and you probably don't either.)

THE POOR MAN - Some kind of really grungy jerkin, barefoot. Should look like a fifteenth century street person.

THE QUARTETTE - Traditional Normal Rockwell caroling clothing. bright coats, stocking caps, scarves.

None of these suggestions are written in stone. Use your imagination and costuming the play may be one of the most enjoyable parts of the production.

PROPS

Lying on stage, right. Sticks, propane tank and charcoal briquet sack which the poor man will pick up when "gathering fu-u-el."

SCRUFFY - Pouch with "snow dome" in it which he carries on his belt. Plastic knife in sheath on his belt. Later in play, the scroll. And THE SACK. This is the most important prop in the play. It must be enormous. It is simply made by buying brightly colored burlap (or brown burlap, if you're a purist), about four feet wide, about sixteen feet long, and then doubling it and sewing up the sides. The sack is then filled with balloons and crumpled newspapers to give it volume but no real weight and tied at the top.

THE POOR MAN - A small burlap sack.

SIR EWING - A plastic sword and scabbard. A stick horse. (or you can forgo the horse and just use a method similar to the Monty Python form of riding. If you don't know what that is, get the cassette of "Monty Python and the Holy Grail.")

SISTER ANTAGONISTICA - a tambourine with which she solicits alms.

THE BUREAUCRAT - A clipboard, or possibly some kind of small computer datebook. A large sheaf of forms.

LIGHTING AND SOUND

If you have the capacity, the play should probably open with blue lights, very gradually bringing in the whites until all actors are easily seen, but there is still a suggestion of "night." The throne room would be in full white, as would the first optional epilogue. The second optional epilogue would be under blue lights. If you can't do this, just turn your lights off and on.

If you have a public address system, you will want to use "wind" sounds at various points in the play to indicate how "cru-el" the night is. You may find these on a sound affects record, but I think it's funnier to just have a person fake the wind sounds rather obviously. Some productions have used recorded instrumental versions of "Good King Wenceslas" before and after the show.

NOTES FOR THE DIRECTOR
(Especially the amateur director.)

Experienced directors will probably stop reading rather shortly into this section. First, the accents. The play is written to be done with British accents and this will enhance the humor considerably. (Anything is funnier done with a British accent-- at least Americans think so.) Since the accents don't have to be particularly authentic, many people can do this, even older children (who've spent a lot of time watching television). If only some your cast can do the accents, it's most important that the King, Scruffy, the Two Peasants, and Sir Ewing have accents, so keep this in mind when casting. If you want to complicate things more, The King, Sir Ewing, Sister Antagonistica, and Burgher Morgan should speak with "cultured" British accents while Scruffy, the two peasants, and The Poor Man should do Cockney. You can flip a coin for The Bureaucrat. If you can't help your cast with the accents, try to find someone who can.

This is satirical farce and the parts should be "overacted." The King should be somewhat controlled, but often "posing" with elaborate, stylized gestures. Sir Ewing is Sir Lawrence Olivier out of control, chewing up the Shakespearean scenery, striding melodramatically back and forth across the stage, waving his arms (And his sword.) heroically. Sister Antagonistica simpers, Burgher Morgan is bombastic, The Bureaucrat is an officious weasel. Only Scruffy is somewhat withdrawn from all this, the traditional "wise fool," regarding the behavior of his supposed superiors with tired cynicism.

Three final tips for amateur directors. First, if you do not know how to "block" a play, get a book for amateur directors that tells you. (If you're really just getting started, "blocking" is the scheme of movements and gestures and position on stage used by the actors.) Blocking must be carefully worked out in early rehearsals and adhered to in production. Otherwise you wind up with your actors "clumped" to one side of the stage, standing in front of each other, distracting from the more important action, etc. And, if they just stand there, it's boring.

Secondly, cue pick ups. Unless there is a reason for a pause, actors should pick up their lines immediately following their cue line (the previous line of another actor). There should not even be time for them to take a breath after their cue line. Some actors do this naturally, some take a lot of work. If there is too much time between lines, the play becomes boring. (Note and exception. I'm talking about coming in after the line of the previous speaker. I'm not suggesting talking overly rapidly or not pausing within the same actor's speech. The exception is when the audience laughs. If the audience laughs at a line, the next speaker should wait until they are finished. Not waiting may make the audience stop laughing. It is called "killing a laugh" and is the cardinal sin of actors doing a comedy.)

Finally, your actors must be heard. Work with them on this from the beginning. If you can't seem to help them, get that book for amateur directors to learn how.

SPECIAL NOTE

The following program note was included in the program for one production of the play: "The real Wenceslas was not a king and he wasn't British. He was Czechoslovakian and lived in the tenth century A.D. The British accents are used because, well, they're more 'Christmasy.'"

CONCLUDING COMMENT

If you're doing your first play and all this seems too much for you, don't worry about it. I think one of the reasons that "The Ballad of King Windowglass" has been so popular is that casts have had a great time being in a play where they could really "ham it up." And the audiences have enjoyed this too. I don't want to spoil your fun by persuading you to spend too much time worrying about whether you're doing it just right. Of course, I hope you can do it as professionally as possible.

Jack Kurtz

For all enquiries regarding motion picture, television, and other media rights, please contact Samuel French.

MUSIC USE NOTE

Licensees are solely responsible for obtaining formal written permission from copyright owners to use copyrighted music in the performance of this play and are strongly cautioned to do so. If no such permission is obtained by the licensee, then the licensee must use only original music that the licensee owns and controls. Licensees are solely responsible and liable for all music clearances and shall indemnify the copyright owners of the play(s) and their licensing agent, Samuel French, against any costs, expenses, losses and liabilities arising from the use of music by licensees. Please contact the appropriate music licensing authority in your territory for the rights to any incidental music.

IMPORTANT BILLING AND CREDIT REQUIREMENTS

If you have obtained performance rights to this title, please refer to your licensing agreement for important billing and credit requirements.